'IF HE ONLY KNEW
WHAT IT WAS, HE
WOULD FIX IT;
HE WOULD KILL
THIS MEAN THING.'

RALPH ELLISON
Born 1914, Oklahoma City, USA
Died 1994, New York City, USA

'In a Strange Country' was originally published in 1944. 'Boy on a Train', 'Hymie's Bull' and 'The Black Ball' are taken from *Flying Home and Other Stories*, first published in 1996.

ELLISON IN PENGUIN MODERN CLASSICS
Flying Home and Other Stories
Invisible Man
Juneteenth

RALPH ELLISON

The Black Ball

PENGUIN BOOKS

PENGUIN CLASSICS

UK | USA | Canada | Ireland | Australia
India | New Zealand | South Africa

Penguin Books is part of the Penguin Random House group
of companies whose addresses can be found at
global.penguinrandomhouse.com.

Penguin
Random House
UK

All stories taken from *Flying Home and Other Stories*, first published in
the United States of America by Vintage Books, a division of Random
House, Inc. 1996
This selection first published 2018
005

Set in 12/15 pt Dante MT Std
Typeset by Jouve (UK), Milton Keynes
Printed in Great Britain by Clays Ltd, Elcograf S.p.A.

ISBN: 978-0-241-33922-0

www.greenpenguin.co.uk

Contents

Boy on a Train

The train gave a long, shrill, lonely whistle, and seemed to gain speed as it rushed downgrade between two hills covered with trees. The trees were covered with deep-red, brown and yellow leaves. The leaves fell on the side of the hill and scattered down to the gray rocks along the opposite tracks. When the engine blew off steam, the little boys could see the white cloud scatter the colored leaves against the side of the hill. The engine hissed, and the leaves danced in the steam like leaves in a white wind.

'See, Lewis, Jack Frost made the pretty leaves. Jack Frost paints the leaves all the pretty colors. See, Lewis: brown, and purple, and orange, and yellow.'

The little boy pointed and paused after naming each color, his finger bent against the glass of the train window. The baby repeated the colors after him, looking intently for Jack Frost.

It was hot in the train, and the car was too close to the engine, making it impossible to open the window. More than once, cinders found a way into the car and flew into the baby's eyes. The woman raised her head from her book from time to time to watch the little boys. The car was filthy, and part of it was used for baggage. Up front, the pine shipping box of a casket stood in a corner. Wonder what poor soul that is in there, the woman thought.

Bags and trunks covered the floor up front, and now and then the butcher came in to pick up candy, or fruit or magazines, to sell back in the white cars. He would come in and pick up a basket with candy, go out, come back; pick up a basket of fruit, go out; come back, pick up magazines, and on till everything had been carried out; then he would start all over again.

He was a big, fat white man with a red face, and the little boy hoped he would give them a piece of candy; after all, he had so much, and Mama didn't have any nickels to give them. But he never did.

The mother read intently, holding a page in her hand as she scanned, then turned it slowly. They were the only passengers in the section of seats reserved for colored. She turned her head, looking back toward the door leading to the other car; it was time for the butcher to return. Her brow wrinkled annoyedly. The butcher had tried to touch her breasts when she and the boys first came into the car, and she had spat in his face and told him to keep his dirty hands where they belonged. The butcher had turned red and gone hurriedly out of the car, his baskets swinging violently on his arms. She hated him. Why couldn't a Negro woman travel with her two boys without being molested?

The train was past the hills now, and into fields that were divided by crooked wooden fences and that spread rolling and brown with stacks of corn as far as the blue horizon fringed with trees. The fences reminded the boy of the crooked man who walked a crooked mile.

Red birds darted swiftly past the car, ducking down into the field, then shooting up again when you looked back to see the telephone poles and fields turning, and sliding fast away from the train. The boys were having a good time of it. It was their first trip. The countryside was bright gold with Indian summer. Way across a field, a boy was leading a cow by a rope and a dog was barking at the cow's feet. It was a nice dog, the boy on the train thought, a collie. Yes, that was the kind of dog it was – a collie.

A freight was passing, going in the direction of Oklahoma City, passing so swiftly that its orange-and-red cars seemed a streak of watercolor with gray spaces punched through. The boy felt funny whenever he thought of Oklahoma City, like he wanted to cry. Perhaps they would never go back. He wondered what Frank and R.C. and Petey were doing now. Picking peaches for Mr Stewart? A lump rose in his throat. Too bad they had to leave just when Mr Stewart had promised them half of all the peaches they could pick. He sighed. The train whistle sounded very sad and lonesome.

Well, now they were going to McAlester, where Mama would have a nice job and enough money to pay the bills. Gee, Mama must have been a good worker for Mr Balinger to send all the way to Oklahoma City for her to come work for him. Mama was happy to go, and he was glad for Mama to be happy; she worked so hard now that Daddy was gone. He closed his eyes tight, trying to see the picture of Daddy. He must never forget how Daddy looked. He would look like that himself when he grew up: tall and kind and always joking and reading books . . . *Well, just wait; when he got big and carried Mama and Lewis back to Oklahoma City everybody would see how well he took care of Mama, and she would say, 'See, these are my two boys', and would be very proud. And everybody would say, 'See, aren't Mrs Weaver's boys two fine men?' That was the way it would be.*

The thought made him lose some of the lump that came into his throat when he thought of never, never going back, and he turned to see who it was coming through the door.

A white man and a little boy came into the car and walked up front. His mother looked up, then lowered her eyes to her book again. He stood up and looked over the backs of the chairs, trying to see what the man and boy were doing. The white boy held a tiny dog in his arms, stroking its head. The little white boy asked the man to let him take the dog out, but the man said no, and they went, rocking from side to side, out of the car. The dog must have been asleep, because all the time he hadn't made a sound. The little white boy was dressed like the kids you see in moving pictures. Did he have a bike? the boy wondered.

He looked out the window. There were horses

now, a herd of them, running and tossing their manes and tails and pounding the ground all wild when the whistle blew. He saw himself on a white horse, swinging a l-a-r-i-a-t over the broncos' heads and yelling 'Yip, yip, yippee!' like Hoot Gibson in the movies. The horses excited Lewis, and he beat his hands against the window and cried, 'Giddap! Giddap!' The boy smiled and looked at his mother. She was looking up from her page and smiling, too. Lewis was cute, he thought.

They stopped at a country town. Men were standing in front of the station, watching the porter throw off a bunch of newspapers. Then several white men came into the car and one said, 'This must be it,' and pointed to the big box, and the porter said, 'Yeah, this is it all right. It's the only one we got this trip, so this must be the one.' Then the porter jumped out of the car and went into the station. The men were dressed in black suits with white shirts. They seemed very uncomfortable with their high collars, and acted very solemn. They pushed the box over gently and lifted it out the side door of the car. The white men in overalls watched them from the platform. They put the box in a wagon, and the man said 'Giddap' to the horses and they drove away, the men on the back with the box looking very straight and stiff.

One of the men on the platform was picking his teeth and spitting tobacco juice on the ground. The station was painted green, and a sign on the side read TUBE ROSE SNUFF and showed a big white flower; it didn't look like a rose, though. It was hot, and the men had their shirts open at the collar and wore red bandannas around their necks. They were standing in the same position when the train pulled out, staring. Why, he wondered, did white folks stare at you that way?

Outside the town, he saw a big red rock barn standing behind some trees. Beside it stood something he had never seen before. It was high and round and made out of the same kind of rock as the barn. He climbed into his seat and pointed.

'What is that tall thing, Mama?' he said.

She raised her head and looked.

'It's a silo, son,' she said. 'That's where the corn is stored.' Her eyes were strangely distant when she turned her face back to him. The sun slanted across her eyes, and her skin was brown and clear. He eased down into the seat. *Silo, silo. Almost as tall as the*

Colcord Building in Oklahoma City that Daddy helped to build . . .

He jumped, startled; Mama was calling his name with tears in her voice. He turned around and tears were on her face.

'Come around here, James,' she said. 'Bring Lewis.'

He took Lewis by the hand and moved into the seat beside her. *What had they done?*

'James, son,' she said. 'That old silo back there's been here a long time. It made me remember when years ago me and your daddy came over this same old Rock Island line on our way to Oklahoma City. We had just been married and was very happy going west because we had heard that colored people had a chance out here.'

James smiled, listening; he loved to hear Mama tell about when she and Daddy were young, and about what they used to do down South. Yet he felt this was to be something different. Something in Mama's voice was vast and high, like a rainbow; yet something sad and deep, like when the organ played in church, was around Mama's words.

'Son, I want you to remember this trip,' she said.

'You understand, son. I *want* you to remember. You *must*, you've *got* to understand.'

James sensed something; he tried hard to understand. He stared into her face. Tears were glistening in her eyes, and he felt he would cry himself. He bit his lip. No, he was the man of the family, and he couldn't act like the baby. He swallowed, listening.

'You remember this, James,' she said. 'We came all the way from Georgia on this same railroad line fourteen years ago, so things would be better for you children when you came. You must remember this, James. We traveled far, looking for a better world, where things wouldn't be so hard like they were down South. That was fourteen years ago, James. Now your father's gone from us, and you're the man. Things are hard for us colored folks, son, and it's just us three alone and we have to stick together. Things is hard, and we have to fight . . . O Lord, we have to fight! . . .'

She stopped, her lips pressed tight together as she shook her head, overcome with emotion. James placed his arm around her neck and caressed her cheek.

'Yes, Mama,' he said. 'I won't forget.'

He could not get it all, but yet he understood. It

was like understanding what music without words said. He felt very full inside. Now Mama was pulling him close to her; the baby rested against her other side. This was familiar; since Daddy died Mama prayed with them, and now she was beginning to pray. He bowed his head.

'Go with us and keep us, Lord. Then it was me and him, Lord; now it's me and his children. And I'm thankful, Lord. You saw fit to take him, Lord, and it's well with my soul in Thy name. I was happy, Lord; life was like a mockingbird a-singing. And all I ask now is to stay with these children, to raise them and protect them, Lord, till they're old enough to go their way. Make them strong and unafraid, Lord. Give them strength to meet this world. Make them brave to go where things is better for our people, Lord . . .'

James sat with head bowed. Always when Mama prayed, he felt tight and smoldering inside. And he kept remembering his father's face. He could not remember Daddy ever praying, but Daddy's voice had been deep and strong when he sang in the choir on Sunday mornings. James wanted to cry, but, vaguely, he felt *something* should be punished for making Mama cry. Something cruel had made her cry. He felt the tightness in his throat becoming anger. If he only knew what it was, he would fix it; he would kill this mean thing that made Mama feel so bad. It must have been awful because Mama was strong and brave and even killed mice when the white woman she used to work for only raised her dress and squealed like a girl, afraid of them. If he only knew what it was . . . Was it God?

'Please keep us three together in this strange town, Lord. The road is dark and long and my sorrows heavy but, if it be Thy will, Lord, let me educate my boys. Let me raise them so they'll be better able to live this life. I don't want to live for myself, Lord, just for these boys. Make them strong, upright men, Lord; make them fighters. And when my work on earth is done, take me home to Thy kingdom, Lord, safe in the arms of Jesus.'

He heard her voice trail off to a tortured moan behind her trembling lips. Tears streamed down her face. James was miserable; he did not like to see Mama cry, and turned his eyes to the window as she began wiping away the tears. He was glad she was through now because the butcher would be coming back into the car in a few minutes. He did not want a white man to see Mama cry.

They were crossing a river now. The slanting girders of a bridge moved slowly past the train. The river was muddy and red, rushing along beneath them. The train stopped, and the baby was pointing to a cow on the banks of the river below. The cow stood gazing out over the water, chewing her cud – looking like a cow in the baby's picture book, only there were no butterflies about her head.

'Bow-wow!' the baby said. Then, questioningly: 'Bow-wow?'

'No, Lewis, it's a cow,' James said. 'Moo,' he said. 'Cow.' The baby laughed, delighted. 'Moo-oo.' He was very interested.

James watched the water. The train was moving again, and he wondered why his mother cried. It wasn't just that Daddy was gone; it didn't sound just that way. It was something else. I'll kill it when I get big, he thought. I'll make it cry just like it's making Mama cry!

The train was passing an oil field. There were many wells in the field; and big round tanks, gleaming like silver in the sun. One well was covered with boards and looked like a huge Indian wigwam against the sky. The wells all pointed straight up at the sky. Yes, I'll kill it. I'll make it cry. Even if it's God, I'll make God cry, he thought. I'll kill Him; I'll kill God and not be sorry!

The train jerked, gaining speed, and the wheels began clicking a ragged rhythm to his ears. There were many advertising signs in the fields they were rolling past. All the signs told about the same things for sale. One sign showed a big red bull and read BULL DURHAM.

'Moo-oo,' the baby said.

James looked at his mother; she was through crying now, and she smiled. He felt some of his tightness ebb away. He grinned. He wanted very much to kiss her, but he must show the proper reserve of a man now. He grinned. Mama was beautiful when she smiled. He made a wish never to forget what she had said. 'This is 1924, and I'll never forget it,' he whispered to himself. Then he looked out the window, resting his chin on the palm of his hand, wondering how much farther they would have to ride, and if there would be any boys to play football in McAlester.

Hymie's Bull

We were just drifting; going no place in particular, having long ago given up hopes of finding jobs. We were just knocking around the country. Just drifting, ten black boys on an L & N freight. From Birmingham we had swung up to the world's fair at Chicago, where the bull had met us in the yards and turned us around and knocked a few lumps on our heads as souvenirs. If you've ever had a bull stand so close he can't miss, and hit you across the rump as you crawled across the top of a boxcar and when you tried to get out of the way, because you knew he had a gun as well as a loaded stick, you've had him measure a tender spot on your head and let go with his loaded stick like a man cracking black walnuts with a hammer; and if when you started to climb down the side of the car because you didn't want to jump from the moving train like he said, you've had him step on your fingers with his heavy boots and grind them with his heel like you'd do a cockroach and then if you didn't let go, he beat you across the knuckles with his loaded stick till you did let go; and when you did, you hit the cinders and found yourself tumbling and sliding on your face away from the train faster than the telephone poles alongside the tracks, then you can understand why we were glad as hell we only had a few lumps on the head. Especially when you remember that the Chicago bulls hate black bums 'bout as much as Texas Slim, who'll kill a Negro as quick as he'll crack down on a blackbird sitting on a fence.

Bulls are pretty bad people to meet if you're a bum. They have head-whipping down to a science and they're always ready to go into action. They know all the places to hit to change a bone into jelly, and they seem to feel just the place to kick you to make your backbone feel like it's going to fold up like the old collapsible drinking cups we used when we were kids. Once a bull hit me across the bridge of my nose and I felt like I was coming apart like a cigarette floating in a urinal. They can hit you on your head and bust your shoes.

But sometimes the bulls get the worst of it, and whenever a bull is missing at the end of a run and they find him all cut up and bleeding, they start taking all the black boys off the freights. Most of the time, they don't care who did it, because the main thing is to make some black boy pay for it. Now when you hear that we're the only bums that carry knives you can just put that down as bull talk because what I'm fixing to tell you about was done by an ofay bum named Hymie from Brooklyn.

We were riding a manifest, and Hymie was sick from some bad grub he'd bummed in a little town a few miles back when the freight had stopped for water. Maybe it wasn't the grub; maybe it was the old mulligan pot he'd cooked it in back there in the jungle. We liked that spot because sunflowers grew there and gave plenty of shade from the sun. But anyway, Hymie was sick and riding on top. It was hot and the flies kept swarming into the car so fast that we stopped paying them no mind. Hymie must have caught hell from them though because his dinner kept coming up and splattering the air. He must have been plenty bothered with the flies because we could see his dinner fly past the door of the car where we were. Once it was very red like a cardinal flying past in the green fields along the tracks. Come to think of it, it might have been a cardinal flying past. Or it might have been something else that smelled like swill from a farmyard.

We tried to get the guy to come down, but he said that he felt better out in the air, so we left him alone. In fact we started to play blackjack for cigarette butts and soon forgot about Hymie; that is, until it had gotten too dark in the boxcar to see the spots on the cards. Then I decided to go out on top to watch the sunset.

The sun was a big globe in the west that seemed to drop away like a basketball toward a basket, and the freight seemed to be trying to catch it before it got there. You could see large swarms of flies following the freight cars like gulls over a boat; only the noise *they* made was lost in the roar of the train. In the field you could see a flock of birds flying away into the sunset, shooting off at an angle to rise and dip, rise and dip, sail and pivot in the wind like kites cut loose from their strings.

I stood on top, feeling the wind pushing against my eyes and whipping my pants against my legs, and waved to Hymie. He had his legs locked around the open ventilator of a refrigerator car hooked next to ours. In that light he looked like a fellow propped in a corner with his hands and feet tied like in a gangster picture. I waved to Hymie, and he waved back. It was a weak wave. The train was going downgrade now, and the fields passed in a curve, and it made you feel like you were on a merry-go-round. When you tried to holler, your voice was small, like the sound you heard when you used to sit on the bottom of the swimming hole and knock rocks together. So we, Hymie and me, just waved.

I felt sorry for the poor guy out there alone. I wished there was something I could do for him, but they don't have water on side-door Pullmans and I guess bums are too dumb to carry canteens. Then I thought, To heck with Hymie. A few miles down the road when we got South, he and the other guys would go into another car anyway.

I stood there on top listening to the rhythm of the wheels bumping along the tracks. Sometimes the rhythm was even, like kids in Harlem beating empty boxes around a bonfire at nightfall as they play along the curbs. I stood there on top listening, bent slightly forward to keep my balance like a guy skiing, and thought of my mother. I had left her two months before, not even knowing that I would ever hop freights. Poor Mama, she had tried hard to keep my brother and me at home, but she fed us too long alone, and we were getting much too grown-up to let her do it any longer, so we left home looking for jobs.

It was now becoming almost too dark to see, when all at once the freight gave a jerk, and every boxcar in the train started racing every other car bumpty-bump down the tracks to the engine like they were meant to knock it into a faster speed when they got there. Then I looked down to where Hymie was riding, and there was a bull crawling toward him with a stick in his hand. I hollered for Hymie to watch out, but the noise swallowed up my voice and the bull was drawing closer all the time. You see, Hymie was asleep, his legs still locked around the ventilator, when the bull reached him. Then the bull grabs Hymie to yank him up and starts lamming with his stick at the same time. Hymie woke up fighting and yelling; I could see his face. The stick would land, and a scream would drift back to where I crawled, almost too excited to move. The freight streaked along like a long black dog, and up on top we were like three monkeys clinging to his back, like you see sometimes at a circus. The bull finally got his knees on Hymie's chest and was choking him, the stick hanging from his wrist by a leather thong.

Sometimes he tried to break Hymie's hold to throw him off the car, and sometimes he lammed away with the loaded stick. Hymie fought the bull the best he could, but he fumbled in his pocket with one hand at the same time. You could see the bull hit, measure and hit, and Hymie kept his left hand in the bull's face and all the time he was fumbling in his pocket.

Then I saw something flash in the fast-fading light, and Hymie went into action with his blade. The bull was still hammering away with his stick when Hymie started cutting him aloose. You could see the knife flash up past Hymie's head and then dive down and across both the bull's wrists, and you could hear him scream because all the time you were coming closer and you could see him let Hymie go and Hymie raise himself, swing the blade around in half-circles like a snake and the blade swing back around as though measuring just the right spot, then dive into the bull's throat. Hymie pulled the knife around from ear to ear in the bull's throat; then he stabbed him and pushed him off the top of the car. The bull paused a second in the air like a kid diving off a trestle into a river, then hit the cinders below. Something was warm on my face, and I found that some of the bull's blood had blown back like spray when a freight stops to take on water from a tank.

It was dark now, and Hymie tore off his top shirt, and dropped it over the edge of the car, and crawled down the side. He hung there until the train hit an upgrade and slowed down. We were coming to a little town on a hill. Lights were scattered here and there like raisins in a cake, and drawing nearer I saw Hymie grow tense and fall clear of the car. He hit the dirt hard, rolled a few yards, and got up to his feet. By then we were too far gone to see him in the dim light. We rolled past the little town, and the whistle screamed its lonely sound and I wondered if that was the last I'd see of Hymie . . .

I heard later on that the shirt Hymie wore was found caught on a field fence and that his switchblade was still sticking in the bull. The bull had rolled from the cinders into the vines which lined the tracks, and lay there all bloody among the flowers that looked like tiger lilies.

The next day about dusk we were pulling into the yards at Montgomery, Alabama, miles down the line, and got the scare of our lives. The train had to cross a trestle before it could reach the yards. It was going slow, and as soon as it crossed we started getting off. All at once we heard someone hollering, and when we ran up to the front of the freight, there were two bulls, a long one and a short one, fanning heads with their gun barrels. They were making everybody line up so they could see us better. The sky was cloudy and very black. We knew Hymie's bull had been found and some black boy had to go. But luck must've been with us this time because just then the storm broke and the freight started to pull out of the yards. The bulls hollered for no one to get back on the train and we broke and ran between some cars on around to try to catch the freight pulling out at the other end of the yards. We made it. We rode up on top that night out in the rain. It was uncomfortable, but we were happy as hell, and we knew the sun would dry our clothes on us the next day, and we would grab something fast going far away from where Hymie got his bull.

The Black Ball

I had rushed through the early part of the day mopping the lobby, placing fresh sand in the tall green jars, sweeping and dusting the halls, and emptying the trash to be burned later on in the day into the incinerator. And I had stopped only once to chase out after a can of milk for Mrs Johnson, who had a new baby and who was always nice to my boy. I had started at six o'clock, and around eight I ran out to the quarters where we lived over the garage to dress the boy and give him his fruit and cereal. He was very thoughtful sitting there in his high chair and paused several times with his spoon midway to his mouth to watch me as I chewed my toast.

'What's the matter, son?'

'Daddy, am I black?'

'Of course not, you're brown. You know you're not black.'

'Well, yesterday Jackie said I was so black.'

'He was just kidding. You musn't let them kid you, son.'

'Brown's much nicer than white, isn't it, Daddy?'

He was four, a little brown boy in blue rompers, and when he talked and laughed with imaginary playmates, his voice was soft and round in its accents like those of most Negro Americans.

'Some people think so. But American is better than both, son.'

'Is it, Daddy?'

'Sure it is. Now forget this talk about you being black, and Daddy will be back as soon as he finishes his work.'

I left him to play with his toys and a book of pictures until I returned. He was a pretty nice fellow, as he used to say after particularly quiet afternoons while I tried to study, and for which quietness he expected a treat of candy or a 'picture movie', and I often left him alone while I attended to my duties in the apartments.

I had gone back and started doing the brass on the front doors when a fellow came up and stood watching from the street. He was lean and red in the face with that redness that comes from a long diet of certain foods. You see much of it in the deep South, and here in the Southwest it is not uncommon. He stood there watching, and I could feel his eyes in my back as I polished the brass.

I gave special attention to that brass because for Berry, the manager, the luster of these brass panels and door handles was the measure of all my industry. It was near time for him to arrive.

'Good morning, John,' he would say, looking not at me but at the brass.

'Good morning, sir,' I would say, looking not at him but at the brass. Usually his face was reflected there. For him, I *was* there. Besides that brass, his money, and the half-dozen or so plants in his office, I don't believe he had any other real interests in life.

There must be no flaws this morning. Two fellows who worked at the building across the street had already been dismissed because whites had demanded their jobs, and with the boy at that age needing special foods and me planning to enter school again next term, I couldn't afford to allow something like that out on the sidewalk to spoil my chances. Especially since Berry had told one of my friends in the building that he didn't like that 'damned educated nigger'.

I was so concerned with the brass that when the fellow spoke, I jumped with surprise.

'Howdy,' he said. The expected drawl was there. But something was missing, something usually behind that kind of drawl.

'Good morning.'

'Looks like you working purty hard over that brass.'

'It gets pretty dirty overnight.'

That part wasn't missing. When they did have something to say to us, they always became familiar.

'You been working here long?' he asked, leaning against the column with his elbow.

'Two months.'

I turned my back to him as I worked.

'Any other colored folks working here?'

'I'm the only one,' I lied. There were two others. It was none of his business anyway.

'Have much to do?'

'I have enough,' I said. Why, I thought, doesn't he go on in and ask for the job? Why bother me? Why tempt me to choke him? Doesn't he know we aren't afraid to fight his kind out this way?

As I turned, picking up the bottle to pour more polish into my rag, he pulled a tobacco sack from the pocket of his old blue coat. I noticed his hands were scarred as though they had been burned.

'Ever smoke Durham?' he asked.

'No thank you,' I said.

He laughed.

'Not used to anything like that, are you?'

'Not used to what?'

A little more from this guy and I would see red.

'Fellow like me offering a fellow like you something besides a rope.'

I stopped to look at him. He stood there smiling with the sack in his outstretched hand. There were many wrinkles around his eyes, and I had to smile in return. In spite of myself I had to smile.

'Sure you won't smoke some Durham?'

'No thanks,' I said.

He was fooled by the smile. A smile couldn't change things between my kind and his.

'I'll admit it ain't much,' he said. 'But it's a helluva lot different.'

I stopped the polishing again to see what it was he was trying to get after.

'But,' he said, 'I've got something really worth a lot; that is, if you're interested.'

'Let's hear it,' I said.

Here, I thought, is where he tries to put one over on old 'George'.

'You see, I come out from the union and we intend to organize all the building-service help in this district. Maybe you been reading 'bout it in the papers?'

'I saw something about it, but what's it to do with me?'

'Well, first place we'll make 'em take some of this work off you. It'll mean shorter hours and higher wages, and better conditions in general.'

'What you really mean is that you'll get in here and bounce me out. Unions don't want Negro members.'

'You mean *some* unions don't. It used to be that way, but things have changed.'

'Listen, fellow. You're wasting your time and mine. Your damn unions are like everything else in the country – for whites only. What ever caused *you* to give a damn about a Negro anyway? Why should *you* try to organize Negroes?'

His face had become a little white.

'See them hands?'

He stretched out his hands.

'Yes,' I said, looking not at his hands but at the color draining from his face.

'Well, I got them scars in Macon County, Alabama, for saying a colored friend of mine was somewhere else on a day he was supposed to have raped a woman. He was, too, 'cause I was with him. Me and him was trying to borrow some seed fifty miles away when it happened – if it did happen. They made them scars with a gasoline torch and run me out the county 'cause they said I tried to help a nigger make a white woman out a lie. That same night they lynched him and burned down his house. They did that to him and this to me, and both of us was fifty miles away.'

He was looking down at his outstretched hands as he talked.

'God,' was all I could say. I felt terrible when I looked closely at his hands for the first time. It must have been hell. The skin was drawn and puckered and looked as though it had been fried. Fried hands.

'Since that time I learned a lot,' he said. 'I been at this kinda thing. First it was the croppers, and when they got to know me and made it too hot, I quit the country and came to town. First it was in Arkansas and now it's here. And the more I move around, the more I see, and the more I see, the more I work.'

He was looking into my face now, his eyes blue in his red skin. He was looking very earnestly. I said nothing. I didn't know what to say to that. Perhaps he was telling the truth; I didn't know. He was smiling again.

'Listen,' he said. 'Now, don't you go trying to figger it all out right now. There's going to be a series of meetings at this number starting tonight, and I'd like mighty much to see you there. Bring any friends along you want to.'

He handed me a card with a number and 8 P.M. sharp written on it. He smiled as I took the card and made as if to shake my hand but turned and walked down the steps to the street. I noticed that he limped as he moved away.

'Good morning, John,' Mr Berry said. I turned, and there he stood; derby, long black coat, stick, nose glasses and all. He stood gazing into the brass like the wicked queen into her looking glass in the story which the boy liked so well.

'Good morning, sir,' I said.

I should have finished long before.

'Did the man I saw leaving wish to see me, John?'

'Oh no, sir. He only wished to buy old clothes.'

Satisfied with my work for the day, he passed inside, and I walked around to the quarters to look after the boy. It was near twelve o'clock.

I found the boy pushing a toy back and forth beneath a chair in the little room which I used for a study.

'Hi, Daddy,' he called.

'Hi, son,' I called. 'What are you doing today?'

'Oh, I'm trucking.'

'I thought you had to stand up to truck.'

'Not that kind, Daddy, this kind.'

He held up the toy.

'Ooh,' I said. '*That* kind.'

'Aw, Daddy, you're kidding. You always kid, don't you, Daddy?'

'No. When you're bad I don't kid, do I?'

'I guess not.'

In fact, he wasn't – only enough to make it unnecessary for me to worry because he wasn't.

The business of trucking soon absorbed him, and

I went back to the kitchen to fix his lunch and to warm up the coffee for myself.

The boy had a good appetite, so I didn't have to make him eat. I gave him his food and settled into a chair to study, but my mind wandered away, so I got up and filled a pipe hoping that would help, but it didn't, so I threw the book aside and picked up Malraux's *Man's Fate*, which Mrs Johnson had given me, and tried to read it as I drank a cup of coffee. I had to give that up also. Those hands were on my brain, and I couldn't forget that fellow.

'Daddy,' the boy called softly; it's always softly when I'm busy.

'Yes, son.'

'When I grow up I think I'll drive a truck.'

'You do?'

'Yes, and then I can wear a lot of buttons on my cap like the men that bring the meat to the grocery. I saw a colored man with some today, Daddy. I looked out the window, and a colored man drove the truck today, and, Daddy, he had two buttons on his cap. I could see 'em plain.'

He had stopped his play and was still on his knees, beside the chair in his blue overalls. I closed the book and looked at the boy a long time. I must have looked queer.

'What's the matter, Daddy?' he asked. I explained that I was thinking, and got up and walked over to stand looking out the front window. He was quiet for a while; then he started rolling his truck again.

The only nice feature about the quarters was that they were high up and offered a view in all directions. It was afternoon and the sun was brilliant. Off to the side, a boy and girl were playing tennis in a driveway. Across the street a group of little fellows in bright sunsuits were playing on a long stretch of lawn before a white stone building. Their nurse, dressed completely in white except for her dark glasses, which I saw when she raised her head, sat still as a picture, bent over a book on her knees. As the children played, the wind blew their cries over to where I stood, and as I watched, a flock of pigeons swooped down into the driveway near the stretch of green, only to take flight again wheeling in a mass as another child came skipping up the drive pulling some sort of toy. The children saw him and were running toward him in a group when the nurse looked up and called them back. She called something to the child and pointed back in the direction of the garages where he had just come from. I could see him turn slowly around and drag his toy, some kind of bird that flapped its wings like an eagle, slowly after him. He stopped and pulled a flower from one of the bushes that lined the drive, turning to look hurriedly at the nurse, and then ran back down the drive. The child had been Jackie, the little son of the white gardener who worked across the street.

As I turned away I noticed that my boy had come to stand beside me.

'What you looking at, Daddy?' he said.

'I guess Daddy was just looking out on the world.'

Then he asked if he could go out and play with his ball, and since I would soon have to go down myself to water the lawn, I told him it would be all right. But he couldn't find the ball; I would have to find it for him.

'All right now,' I told him. 'You stay in the back out of everybody's way, and you mustn't ask anyone a lot of questions.'

I always warned about the questions, even though it did little good. He ran down the stairs, and soon I could hear the *bump bump bump* of his ball bouncing against the garage doors underneath. But since it didn't make a loud noise, I didn't ask him to stop.

I picked up the book to read again, and must have fallen asleep immediately, for when I came to it was almost time to go water the lawn. When I got downstairs the boy was not there. I called, but no answer. Then I went out into the alley in back of the garages to see if he was playing there. There were three older white boys sitting talking on a pile of old packing cases. They looked uneasy when I came up. I asked if they had seen a little Negro boy, but they said they hadn't. Then I went farther down the alley behind the grocery store where the trucks drove up, and asked one of the fellows working there if he had seen my boy. He said he had been working on the platform all afternoon and that he was sure the boy had not been there. As I started away, the four o'clock whistle blew and I had to go water the lawn. I wondered where the boy could have gone. As I came back up the alley I was becoming alarmed. Then it occurred to me that he might have gone out in front in spite of my warning not to. Of course, that was where he would go, out in front to sit on the grass. I laughed at myself for becoming alarmed and decided not to punish him, even though Berry had given instructions that he was not to be seen out in the front without me. A boy that size will make you do that.

As I came around the building past the tall new evergreens, I could hear the boy crying in just that note no other child has, and when I came completely around I found him standing looking up into a window with tears on his face.

'What is it, son?' I asked. 'What happened?'

'My ball, my ball, Daddy. My ball,' he cried, looking up at the window.

'Yes, son. But what about the ball?'

'He threw it up in the window.'

'Who did? Who threw it, son? Stop crying and tell Daddy about it.'

He made an effort to stop, wiping the tears away with the back of his hand.

'A big white boy asked me to throw him my ball an', an' he took it and threw it up in that window and ran,' he said, pointing.

I looked up just as Berry appeared at the window. The ball had gone into his private office.

'John, is that your boy?' he snapped.

He was red in the face.

'Yessir, but –'

'Well, he's taken his damned ball and ruined one of my plants.'

'Yessir.'

'You know he's got no business around here in front, don't you?'

'Yes!'

'Well, if I ever see him around here again, you're going to find yourself behind the black ball. Now get him on round to the back and then come up here and clean up this mess he's made.'

I gave him one long hard look and then felt for the boy's hand to take him back to the quarters. I had a hard time seeing as we walked back, and scratched myself by stumbling into the evergreens as we went around the building.

The boy was not crying now, and when I looked down at him, the pain in my hand caused me to notice that it was bleeding. When we got upstairs, I sat the boy in a chair and went looking for iodine to doctor my hand.

'If anyone should ask me, young man, I'd say your face needed a good washing.'

He didn't answer then, but when I came out of the bathroom, he seemed more inclined to talk.

'Daddy, what did that man mean?'

'Mean how, son?'

'About a black ball. You know, Daddy.'

'Oh – that.'

'You know, Daddy. What'd he mean?'

'He meant, son, that if your ball landed in his office again, Daddy would go after it behind the old black ball.'

'Oh,' he said, very thoughtful again. Then, after a while he told me: 'Daddy, that white man can't see very good, can he, Daddy?'

'Why do you say that, son?'

'Daddy,' he said impatiently. 'Anybody can see my ball is white.'

For the second time that day I looked at him a long time.

'Yes, son,' I said. 'Your ball *is* white.' Mostly white, anyway, I thought.

'Will I play with the black ball, Daddy?'

'In time, son,' I said. 'In time.'

He had already played with the ball; that he would discover later. He was learning the rules of the game already, but he didn't know it. Yes, he would play with the ball. Indeed, poor little rascal, he would play until he grew sick of playing. My, yes, the old ball game. But I'd begin telling him the rules later.

My hand was still burning from the scratch as I dragged the hose out to water the lawn, and looking down at the iodine stain, I thought of the fellow's fried hands, and felt in my pocket to make sure I still had the card he had given me. Maybe there was a color other than white on the old ball.

In a Strange Country

In the pub his eye had begun to close. White spots danced before him, and he had to cover the eye with his hand in order to see Mr Catti. Mr Catti was drinking now, and as the bottom of the glass swung down and tapped the table, he looked into Mr Catti's pale, sharp-nosed face and smiled. Mr Catti had been very kind, and he was trying hard to be pleasant.

'You miss this on a ship,' he said, draining his glass.

'Do you like our Welsh ale?'

'Very much.'

'It's not so good as before the war,' Mr Catti said sadly.

'It must have been very good,' he said.

He looked guardedly at the pretty, blue-aproned barmaid, seeing her dark hair shift lazily forward as she drew beer from a pump such as he'd seen only in English pictures. With his eye covered he saw much better. Across the room, near the fireplace with its grate of glowing coals, two men were seeing who could knock over a set of skittlepins. One of them started singing 'Treat Me Like an Irish Soldier' as Mr Catti said:

'Have you been long in Wales?'

'About forty-five minutes,' he said.

'Then you have much to see,' Mr Catti said, getting up and carrying the glasses over to the bar to be refilled.

No, he thought, looking at the GUINNESS IS GOOD FOR YOU signs, I've seen enough. Coming ashore from the ship he had felt the excited expectancy of entering a strange land. Moving along the road in the dark he had planned to stay ashore all night, and in the morning he would see the country with fresh eyes, like those with which the Pilgrims had seen the New World. That hadn't seemed so silly then – not until the soldiers bunched at the curb had seemed to spring out of the darkness. Someone had cried, 'Jesus H. Christ,' and he had thought, He's from home, and grinned and apologized into the light they flashed in his eyes. He had felt the blow coming when they yelled, 'It's a goddamn nigger,' but it struck him anyway. He was having a time of it when some of Mr Catti's countrymen stepped in and Mr Catti had guided him into the pub. Now, over several rounds of ale, they had introduced themselves, had discreetly avoided mentioning his eye, and, while he heard with forced attention something of Welsh national history, he had been adjusting himself to the men in cloth caps and narrow-brimmed hats who talked so quietly over their drinks.

At first he had included them in his blind rage. But they had seemed so genuinely and uncondescendingly polite that he was disarmed. Now the anger and resentment had slowly ebbed, and he felt only a smoldering sense of self-hate and ineffectiveness. Why should he blame them when they had only helped him? *He* had been the one so glad to hear an American voice. You can't take it out on them, they're a different breed; even from the English. That's what he's been telling you, he thought, seeing Mr Catti returning, his head held to one side to avoid the smoke from his cigarette, the foam-headed glasses caged in his fingers.

'It's a disgrace to our country, Mr Parker!' Mr Catti said heatedly. 'How is your eye?'

'It's better, thanks,' he said, brightening. 'And don't worry, it's a sort of family quarrel. Are there many like me in Wales?'

'Oh yes! Yanks all over the place. Black Yanks and white.'

'Black *Yanks?*' He wanted to smile.

'Yes. And many a fine lad at that.'

Mr Catti was looking at his wristwatch.

'My, my! I'm sorry, but it's time for my concert. Perhaps you would like to come? The boys at my club are singing – no professionals, mind you, but some very fine voices.'

'No . . . no, I'd better not,' he said. Yet all music was a passion with him, and his interest was aroused.

'It's a private club,' Mr Catti said reassuringly. 'Open only to members – and to our guests, of course. We'd be very glad to have you. Perhaps the boys will sing some of your spirituals.'

'Oh! So you know our music, too?'

'Very well,' Mr Catti said. 'And since your boys have been with us we've learned that, like ourselves, your people love music.'

'I think I'd like very much to go,' he said, rising

and getting into his seaman's topcoat. 'You might
have to guide me along though.'

'Righto. It isn't far. Just a bit up Straight Street.'

Outside, the pale beam of a flashlight revealed the
stone walk. Somewhere in the damp darkness a group
of adolescent girls were singing a nostalgic Tin Pan
Alley tune. Here you go again, he thought. Better go
back to the ship, no telling what'll jump out of the
darkness next; maybe the Second Avenue El. And
suppose someone else brings a Yank? Why spoil the
fun? Hell, so let *him* walk out . . .

Mr Catti was guiding him into a doorway toward
a soft murmur of voices. Maybe, he thought, you'll
hear that old 'spiritual' classic *Massa's in de – Massa's
in de Old Cold Masochism!*

When the light struck his injured eye, it was as
though it were being peeled by an invisible hand. He
did not know whether to cover it or to let it be so as
not to attract attention. What was the use?

Mr Catti was greeting the men who made room
for them at the bar. Looking across the room, where
folding chairs were grouped neatly around rows of
small tables, he heard a man in a blue suit running

brilliant arpeggios upon an upright piano. It was a cheerful room.

'Two whiskeys, Alf,' said Mr Catti to the man behind the bar.

'Right! And a good evening to you, Twm,' the man said.

'This is Mr Parker, Alf,' Mr Catti said, introducing him. 'Mr Parker, Mr Triffit, our club manager.'

'How do you do?' he said, shaking Mr Triffit's hand.

'Welcome to our club, sir,' Mr Triffit said. 'You are an American, I take it?'

'Yes,' he said. And with sly amusement he added, 'A black Yank.'

'I thought Mr Parker would like the concert, Alf. So I brought him along.'

'We're happy to have you, sir,' Mr Triffit said. 'I believe you will enjoy it, Mr Parker. If I do say so myself, our boys are . . . are . . . yes, dammit, they're smashing!'

'I'm sure they are,' he said, thinking, He acts like he'd fight over it.

'Here's all the best,' said Mr Catti.

'Your health, sir,' said Mr Triffit.

45

'To Wales,' Mr Parker said, 'and to you both.'

'And to America, God bless her,' Mr Triffit said.

'Yes,' said Mr Parker, 'and to America.'

He could see Mr Triffit about to mention his eye, and was glad Mr Catti was moving away.

'Come, Mr Parker. We'd better select our seats.'

They sat near the front, where the singers were grouping themselves to begin. The warmth of the liquor was spreading slowly through him now, and it was with a growing sense of remoteness that he heard the first number announced, a Welsh song to be rendered a cappella. The quiet tuning chord sounded far away. He saw the men set themselves and the conductor raising his hand, then, at the downbeat, the quick, audible intake of breath and the precise attack.

The well-blended voices caught him unprepared. He heard the music's warm richness with pleasurable surprise, and heard, beneath the strange Welsh words, echoes of plain song, like that of Russian folk songs sounding.

'It's wonderful,' he whispered, seeing Mr Catti smile knowingly.

He looked about him. He saw the faces of the

listeners caught in a single spell of communication while they sipped their drinks or puffed their pipes or cigarettes. Slowly the hall was filling with friendly swirls of smoke. They were singing another of their songs now, and though he could not understand the words he felt himself drawn closer to its web of meaning. Then the familiar and hateful emotion of alienation gripped his throat.

'It was a song about Wales?' he asked, soothing his eye.

'Exactly!' exclaimed Mr Catti. 'And the other was about a battle in which we defeated the English. Nothing like music to reveal what's in the heart. You don't need lyrics, really.'

A warm flush dyed Mr Catti's face. He's pleased that I understood, he thought. And as the men sang in hushed tones he felt a growing poverty of spirit. He should have known more of the Welsh, of their history and art. If we only had some of what they have, he thought. They are a much smaller nation than ours would be, yet I can remember no song of ours that's of love of the soil or of country. Nor any song of battle other than those of biblical times. And in his mind's eye he saw a Russian peasant kneeling to kiss the earth and rising wet-eyed to enter into battle with cries of fierce exultation. And he felt now, among these men, hearing their voices, a surge of deep longing to know the anguish and exultation of such love.

'Do you see that fellow with the red face there?' asked Mr Catti.

'Yes.'

'Our leading mine owner.'

'And what are the others?'

'Everything. The tenor on the end is a miner. Mr Jones, in the center there, is a butcher. And the dark man next to him is a union official.'

'You'd never think so from their harmony,' he said, smiling.

'When we sing, we are Welshmen,' Mr Catti said as the next number began.

Parker smiled, aware suddenly of an expansiveness that he had known before only at mixed jam sessions. When we jam, sir, we're Jamocrats! He liked these Welsh. Not even on the ship, where the common danger and a fighting union made for a degree of understanding, did he approach white men so closely.

For that's a unity of economics, he said to himself. And this a unity of music, a 'gut language', the 'food of love'. Go on, fool. Behind that blacked-out eye you can get away with it. Knock yourself out. *All right, I will: Dear Wales, I salute thee. I kiss the lips of thy proud spirit through the fair sounds of thy songs. How's that?* Fine. Slightly mixed in metaphor, but not bad. Give us some more, Othello. *Othello? Indeed, and how odd. But. So: Oh my fair warrior nation, because of thee this little while my chaos is gone again –* Again? Parker, keep to the facts. And remember what they did to Othello. *No, he did it to himself. Couldn't believe in his woman, nor in himself.* I know, so that makes Iago a Fifth Columnist. But what do *you* believe in? *Oh, shut – I believe in music!* Well! *And in what's happening here tonight. I believe . . . I want to believe in this people.* Something was getting out of control. He became on guard. At home he could drown his humanity in a sea of concealed cynicism, and white men would never recognize it. But these men might understand. Perhaps, he felt with vague terror, all evening he had been exposed, blinded by the brilliant light of their deeper humanity, and they had seen him for what he was and for what he should have been. He was sobered. Listening now, he thought, You live on the ship, remember. Down Straight Street, in the dark.

And at home you live in Harlem. Quit letting their liquor throw you, or even their hospitality. Do the State some service, Parker. They won't know it. And if these men should, it doesn't matter. Put out that light, Othello – or do you enjoy being hit with one?

'How is your eye now?' Mr Catti asked.

'Almost completely closed.'

'It's a bloody shame!'

'It's been a wonderful evening though,' he said. 'One of the best I've ever spent.'

'I'm glad you came,' Mr Catti said. 'And so are the boys. They can tell that you appreciate the music, and they're pleased.'

'Here's to singing,' he toasted.

'To singing,' said Mr Catti.

'By the way, let me lend you my torch to find your way back. Just return it to Heath's Bookstore. Anyone will direct you.'

'But you'll need it yourself.'

Mr Catti placed the light upon the table. 'Don't worry,' he said. 'I'm at home. I know the city like my own palm.'

'Thanks,' he said with feeling. 'You're very kind.'

*

When the opening bars were struck, he saw the others pushing back their chairs and standing, and he stood, understanding even as Mr Catti whispered, 'Our national anthem.'

There was something in the music and in the way they held their heads that was strangely moving. He hummed beneath his breath. When it was over he would ask for the words.

But even while he heard the final triumphal chord still sounding, the piano struck up 'God Save the King'. It was not nearly so stirring. Then swiftly modulating they swept into the 'Internationale', to words about an international army. He was carried back to when he was a small boy marching in the streets behind the bands that came to his southern town . . .

Mr Catti had nudged him. He looked up, seeing the conductor looking straight at him, smiling. They were all looking at him. Why, was it his eye? Were they playing a joke? And suddenly he recognized the melody and felt that his knees would give way. It was as though he had been pushed into the horrible foreboding country of dreams and they were enticing him into some unwilled and degrading act, from which only his failure to remember the words would save him. It was all unreal, yet it seemed to have happened before. Only now the melody seemed charged with some vast new meaning which that part of him that wanted to sing could not fit with the old familiar words. And beyond the music he kept hearing the soldiers' voices, yelling as they had when the light struck his eye. He saw the singers still staring, and as though to betray him he heard his own voice singing out like a suddenly amplified radio:

'. . . Gave proof through the night
That our flag was still there . . .'

It was like the voice of another, over whom he had no control. His eye throbbed. A wave of guilt shook him, followed by a burst of relief. For the first time in your whole life, he thought with dreamlike wonder, the words are not ironic. He stood in confusion as the song ended, staring into the men's Welsh faces, not knowing whether to curse them or to return their good-natured smiles. Then the conductor was before him, and Mr Catti was saying, 'You're not such a bad singer yourself, Mr Parker. Is he now, Mr Morcan?'

'Why, if he'd stay in Wales, I wouldn't rest until he joined the club,' Mr Morcan said. 'What about it, Mr Parker?'

But Mr Parker could not reply. He held Mr Catti's flashlight like a club and hoped his black eye would hold back the tears.